Dear Parents:

Congratulations! Your child is taking the first steps on an exciting journey. The destination? Independent reading!

STEP INTO READING® will help your child get there. The program offers five steps to reading success. Each step includes fun stories and colorful art or photographs. In addition to original fiction and books with favorite characters, there are Step into Reading Non-Fiction Readers, Phonics Readers and Boxed Sets, Sticker Readers, and Comic Readers—a complete literacy program with something to interest every child.

Learning to Read, Step by Step!

Ready to Read   Preschool–Kindergarten
• big type and easy words • rhyme and rhythm • picture clues
For children who know the alphabet and are eager to begin reading.

Reading with Help   Preschool–Grade 1
• basic vocabulary • short sentences • simple stories
For children who recognize familiar words and sound out new words with help.

Reading on Your Own   Grades 1–3
• engaging characters • easy-to-follow plots • popular topics
For children who are ready to read on their own.

Reading Paragraphs   Grades 2–3
• challenging vocabulary • short paragraphs • exciting stories
For newly independent readers who read simple sentences with confidence.

Ready for Chapters   Grades 2–4
• chapters • longer paragraphs • full-color art
For children who want to take the plunge into chapter books but still like colorful pictures.

STEP INTO READING® is designed to give every child a successful reading experience. The grade levels are only guides; children will progress through the steps at their own speed, developing confidence in their reading. The F&P Text Level on the back cover serves as another tool to help you choose the right book for your child.

Remember, a lifetime love of reading starts with a single step!

All rights reserved. Published in the United States by Random House Children's Books,
a division of Penguin Random House LLC, New York. Originally published in hardcover
in the United States by Alfred A. Knopf, an imprint of Random House Children's Books,
New York, in 1970. Step into Reading, Random House, and the Random House colophon
are registered trademarks of Penguin Random House LLC.

Visit us on the Web!
StepIntoReading.com
randomhousekids.com
Educators and librarians, for a variety of teaching tools,
visit us at RHTeachersLibrarians.com

Library of Congress Cataloging-in-Publication Data
Lionni, Leo, 1910–1999, author, illustrator.
Fish is fish / Leo Lionni.
pages   cm. — (Step-into-reading)
"Originally published in hardcover in the United States by Alfred A. Knopf in 1970."
Summary: After his friend, the tadpole, becomes a frog and leaves the pond to explore the world,
a little fish decides that maybe he should not remain in the pond either.
ISBN 978-0-553-52218-1 (tr. pbk.) — ISBN 978-0-553-52219-8 (lib. bdg.)
[1. Fishes—Fiction. 2. Frogs—Fiction.] I. Title.
PZ7.L6634Fis 2015
[E]—dc23   2014046729

This book has been officially leveled by using the F&P Text Level Gradient™ Leveling System.
Printed in the United States of America   10 9 8 7 6 5 4 3 2
Random House Children's Books supports the First Amendment and celebrates the right to read.

STEP INTO READING®

3 STEP

READING ON YOUR OWN

Fish
is
Fish

by Leo Lionni

Random House 🏠 New York

4

At the edge of the woods
there was a pond,
and there a minnow
and a tadpole
swam among the weeds.
They were inseparable friends.

One morning the tadpole discovered
that during the night he had
grown two little legs.
"Look," he said triumphantly.
"Look, I am a frog!"
"Nonsense," said the minnow.
"How could you be a frog if only

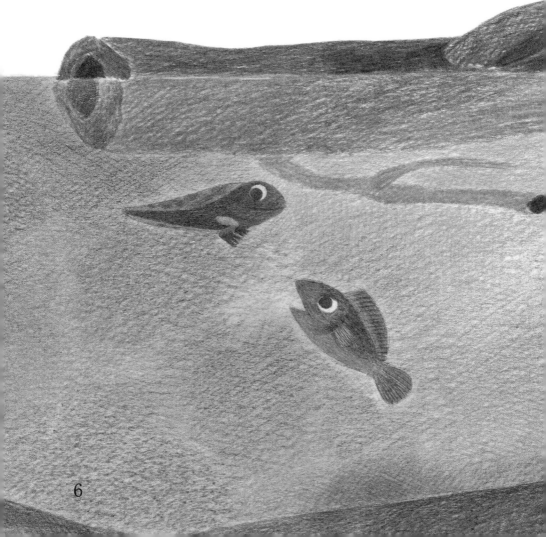

last night you were a little fish,

just like me!"

They argued and argued

until finally the tadpole said,

"Frogs are frogs and fish is fish

and that's that!"

In the weeks that followed,
the tadpole grew tiny front legs

and his tail got smaller
and smaller.

And then one fine day,

a real frog now,

he climbed out of the water
and onto the grassy bank.

The minnow too had grown
and had become
a full-fledged fish.
He often wondered
where his four-footed friend
had gone.
But days and weeks went by
and the frog did not return.

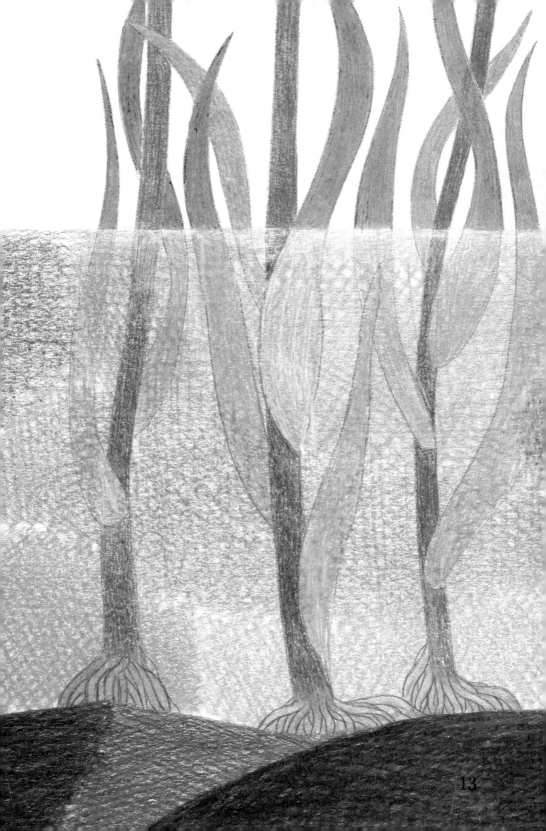

13

Then one day,

with a happy splash that shook

the weeds,

the frog jumped into the pond.

"Where have you been?"

asked the fish excitedly.

"I have been about the world—

hopping here and there,"

said the frog,

"and I have seen

extraordinary things."

"Like what?" asked the fish.

"Birds," said the frog
  mysteriously.

"Birds!" And he told the fish
  about the birds, who had wings,
  and two legs, and many,
  many colors.

As the frog talked,
his friend saw the birds fly
through his mind
like large feathered fish.
"What else?" asked the fish
impatiently.

"Cows," said the frog.

"Cows! They have four legs,

horns, eat grass, and carry

pink bags of milk."

"And people!" said the frog.
"Men, women, children!"
    And he talked and talked
    until it was dark in the pond.

But the picture in the fish's
mind was full of lights
and colors and marvelous
things and he couldn't sleep.
Ah, if he could only jump about
like his friend and see that
wonderful world.

And so the days went by.
The frog had gone and the fish
just lay there dreaming about
birds in flight, grazing cows,

and those strange animals,
all dressed up, that his friend
called people.

One day he finally decided that
come what may,
he too must see them.

And so with a mighty whack of
the tail he jumped clear
out of the water onto the bank.

He landed in the dry,
warm grass and there he lay
gasping for air, unable to
breathe or to move.
"Help," he groaned feebly.

Luckily the frog, who had been
hunting butterflies nearby,
saw him and with all his strength
pushed him back
into the pond.

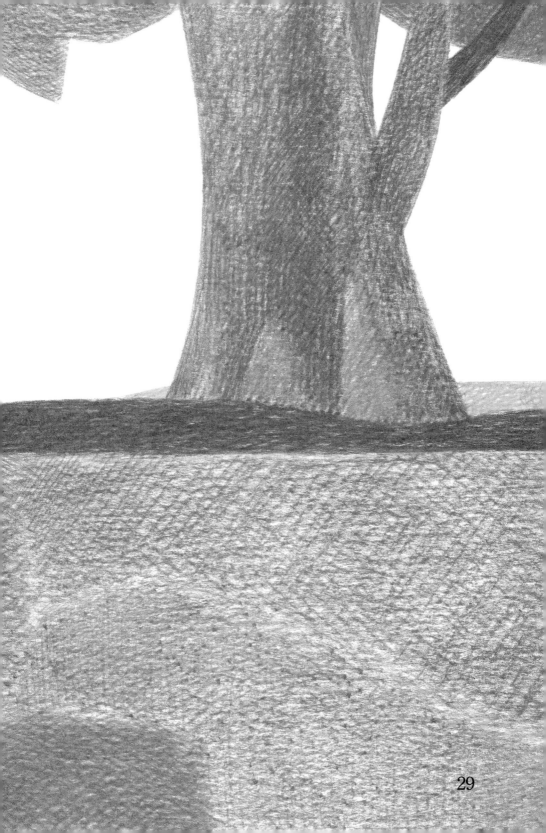

Still stunned, the fish floated about for an instant. Then he breathed deeply, letting the clean cool water run through his gills. Now he felt

weightless again and
with an ever-so-slight
motion of the tail
he could move to and fro,
up and down, as before.

The sunrays reached down
within the weeds and gently
shifted patches of luminous
color. This world was surely
the most beautiful of all worlds.

He smiled at his friend the frog,
who sat watching him from
a lily leaf.
"You were right," he said.
"Fish is fish."

Guess the Word

How well do you know *Fish is Fish*?
Can you remember the story
by reading the sentences below?

1. The minnow and the  swim in the .

2. A tadpole becomes a  when it grows up.

3. The frog describes animals with  called birds.

4. Frogs are frogs and  is fish, but they will always be best friends.

Matching

In this story, the minnow imagines what all the animals look like. Match each animal to its picture.

Minnow

Tadpole

Frog

Bird

What doesn't belong?

Do you remember the pictures from
the story? Which one is different
from the rest?

LEO LIONNI wrote and illustrated more than forty picture books in his lifetime, including four Caldecott Honor Books—*Inch by Inch, Swimmy, Frederick,* and *Alexander and the Wind-Up Mouse.* He died in 1999 at the age of 89.

Praise for Leo Lionni

"If the picture book is a new visual art form
in our time, Leo Lionni is certain to be judged
a master of the genre."

—Selma Lanes, *The New York Times*

When the frogs on Pebble Island find an egg, they're sure it holds a baby chicken . . . until the egg hatches.